Hallow Surprise

Karen Dolby
Illustrated by Alan Marks

Edited by Louie Stowell
Cover design by Will Dawes

Contents

Spook Hall

Some people say that creepy old Spook Hall is haunted. And they're right...

Turn the page for a puzzle-filled adventure.

Keep your eyes open for clues. If you get stuck, there are answers on pages 31 and 32.

The Spookenshivers

Inside this dark and eerie house live a family of ghosts called the Spookenshivers, or Spooks for short – Sam and Sorrel, Ma, Pa and Baby, Grandpa and Grandma and Aunt Serena.

Can you find the seven Spooks? (You can't see Baby. She's asleep inside.)

Ghostographs

Nobody has lived in Spook Hall for years. But the Spookenshivers have haunted the place for centuries and they love their home.

Sir Lancelot Lander ghost hunting

6

The Spooks are always snapping ghostographs for the family album, with their special spooky camera.

Ma and Sorrel cook up some spooky soup.

Pa and Sam check the creeping vine.

Grandma knits (and knits) a scarf.

Grandpa takes a rooftop stroll.

Aunt Serena hanging around with her pet bats.

But the camera also works on living creatures. Sam's brown fruit bat, Bertie, loves playing hide-and-seek...

Can you spot Bertie hiding in one of the pictures?

Gloomy Grandpa

One morning, just before Halloween,
Sorrel heard rattling coming from a
chimney. A cloud of soot whooshed out
and there was a moaning sigh.

Grandpa was sitting on the hearth looking
miserable. "Oh dear! Oh dear," he moaned.
What had upset him? When Sorrel
looked outside, she thought she knew.

Do you know?

"If someone buys the Hall, we'll have to share it with humans," Grandpa sighed. "I remember when the whole place rattled, howled, clanked and groaned with phantoms, and no humans came near. Those were the days!"

Sorrel's plan

When Grandpa floated glumly away, Sorrel said, "Let's throw him a Halloween ball to cheer him up. His birthday's on Halloween."

Sam nodded, and they spent the rest of the day scribbling out invitations.

GRANDPA SPOOKENSHIVERS BIRTHDAY BALL

A ghoulish, ghostly, surprise ball is to be held by the Spookenshivers of Spook Hall.

The party's on Halloween and starts at 8. Wear something haunting for this special spooky date.

"It'll take the Ghost Office weeks to sort through these if we mail them," groaned Sam.

"Don't worry," said Sorrel. "We can deliver them ourselves. We just need to find Grandpa's haunted address book. You know, the blue one with the red ribbon."

Can you spot Grandpa's address book?

Sam and Sorrel set off

Early next morning, the young Spooks
flew off to deliver their invitations. First,
they stopped at some Roman ruins, to give
an invitation to a ghostly Roman centurion
named Quintus. Sorrel pulled out a map
from Grandpa's address book. "The blue
arrow points to Quintus's home," she said.

Where does Quintus live?

Phantom Forest

Quintus said he'd love to come. Next, the children flew on to Phantom Forest.

Quintus

They were looking for a timid tree sprite named Agatha when they bumped into Egbert Eerie, another ghost on the list.

"I wouldn't miss it for the world," he boomed. "Oh, and Agatha lives in the tree stump ringed around with bluebells. It was struck by lightning last month so it's rather black. Poor old Aggie!"

Can you see which tree
stump Agatha lives in?

15

Coffin Castle

When they reached
Agatha's tree stump,
an arm shot out and
grabbed her invitation.

In the distance, Sam
and Sorrel could see the towers and turrets
of Coffin Castle, the home of Grandpa's old
friends the Jesters. The doors were locked –
but ghosts don't need doors to get in.

"Hellooo! We're here to invite
you to our Halloween party!" called Sorrel.

A soft voice answered, "We'll come... if you
can find ussssss."

"Coming, ready or not!" cried Sam, and
they began a game of ghostly hide-and-seek.

Can you find five hidden ghosts?

Dark, dank dungeon

The playful ghosts agreed to come.

"Don't forget Cecil. He's the gloomy ghoul in the dungeon," one called.

Sam and Sorrel slid down slimy stone steps to the darkest, dankest depths of the castle. They spotted Cecil skulking behind a pillar.

"We're here to invite you to our Halloween party," said Sorrel. "Would you like to come?"

"I can't," groaned Cecil. "I've lost my ball and chain. I can't go anywhere without them."

"We'll help you to look," said Sam.

Can you find Cecil's ball and chain?

19

Walter's puzzling path

Next on the list was Walter the water ghost, who haunted a shark-infested lake.

As Sam and Sorrel drew near, a grouchy voice called, "Find your way across the stones. I will NOT talk to you if you fly!"

Can you find a safe path across the lake?

A ghostly trail

Next, after a short flight, they reached their next stop, Forest Farm. But there was no sign of Grandpa's pal Cuthbert who was supposed to live there.

"Boo!" said a voice, making Sam and Sorrel jump.

It was a real, live, small boy.

"Saying boo is our job!" said Sam, huffily.

The boy gave him a cheeky grin. "If you're looking for Cuthbert, you should follow his horse's hoofprints," he said.

Can you see where the hoofprints lead?

The Rolling Bones

Now all the guests were invited, what they needed was some music.

"Grandpa likes really old bands," said Sam. "How about the Rolling Bones? They're thousands of years old."

So they called at the band's studio and found them squabbling. Someone had lost Sid's violin... and Kate's piano... and their music. In fact, lots of things were missing.

Can you spot the missing instruments and music?

25

Spooky supplies

The Rolling Bones agreed to play at Grandpa's Halloween party, and to take good care of their instruments until then.

Sam and Sorrel's final stop was the Party Store, to buy some ghostly decorations.

"We need lightning, mist, shivers, slime, streamers, pumpkin heads and glowing skulls, please," said Sam, as a shiver pierced his foot.

Can you spot everything on their party list?

A surprise party

On Halloween afternoon, Grandma Spook took grumpy Grandpa out for a flight, so that everyone else could make Spook Hall look its ghostly best for his surprise party. When everything was ready, the guests hid.

As Grandpa opened the door, the house
exploded into light and noise. Lightning
flashed and the Rolling Bones struck up a
tune. Everywhere, Grandpa's ghostly friends
appeared chorusing, "Halloween surprise!"

Can you spot all the ghostly guests?

Spooked!

"What a racket!" scowled Grandpa, covering his ears.

The children felt crushed.

But when Grandpa looked out of the window, he grinned. Two terrified humans were being chased away by ghosts.

"I've changed my mind," he chuckled. "This is the best Halloween ever!"

SPOOK HALL FOR SALE

Answers

Pages 4-5
You can see the seven Spooks circled in this picture.

Pages 6-7
Bertie is hiding here among the vine leaves.

Pages 8-9
Grandpa is upset because he has seen a living human outside and a FOR SALE sign.

Pages 10-11
Grandpa's address book is circled here. It is the only blue book with a red ribbon.

Pages 12-13

Quintus lives here.

Pages 14-15
Agatha lives in this tree trunk. It is the only stump that is covered in ivy and blackened, with bluebells growing around it.

Pages 16-17
The five hidden ghosts are circled here.

Pages 18-19
Here are Cecil's ball and chain.

Pages 20-21
The path across to Walter is marked in black.

Pages 22-23
The hoofprints lead to this barn.

Pages 24-25
The missing instruments and music are circled here.

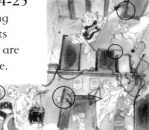

Pages 26-27

Glowing skulls
Slime
Pumpkin heads
Streamers
Lightning
Mist
Shivers

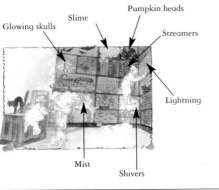

Pages 28-29

Cuthbert
Egbert Eerie
Quintus
Walter
Cecil
Agatha
Creepy Castle Ghosts
The Rolling Bones

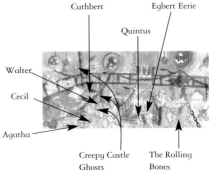

This edition first published in 2007 by Usborne Publishing Ltd., Usborne House, 83-85 Saffron Hill, London EC1N 8RT, England. www.usborne.com Copyright © 2007, 2002, 1995 Usborne Publishing Ltd. The name Usborne and the devices are Trade Marks of Usborne Publishing Ltd. All rights reserved.

No part of this publication may be reproduced, stored in a retrieval system or transmitted in any form or by any means, electronic, mechanical, photocopying, recording or otherwise without the prior permission of the publisher.
Printed in China.
This edition first printed in America 2007. UE